Piper Fox

Shows Kindness

written by Jess Mollo
illustrated by Mark Carnell-Jones

SPARK Publications
Charlotte, NC

Piper Fox Shows Kindness
By Jess Mollo
Illustrated by Mark Carnell-Jones

Designed, produced, and published by SPARK Publications
SPARKpublications.com
Charlotte, North Carolina

Printed in the United States of America.
Hardback, March 2020, ISBN: 978-1-943070-83-1
Paperback, March 2020, ISBN: 978-1-943070-86-2

Piper's heart is kind. Her mind is quick.
With baby Winston, Piper loves to play.

Like any little fox, she likes to help.
She is always looking for a kinder way.

TOY

Baby Winston says,

"I can show kindness like Piper!"

When Piper takes the time
to show some kindness,
it grows and grows
her happy heart!

The happiness that kindness brings is joyful.
The joy becomes the most rewarding part.

“I can show kindness
like Piper!”

She sets the table to prepare for friends.
Helping Mommy is a fun chore.

Piper helps when Daddy's hands are full.
She kindly opens the door.

"I can show kindness
like Piper!"

When friends come over, Piper shares her toys
and hands out cookies while they eat.

She makes her friends feel warm
and welcome here.

By being kind, she makes
the day complete!

“I can show kindness
like Piper!”

When Piper's friends are gone,
it is time to clean, and she
knows just what to do!

She shows kindness by
helping wash the dishes, and
grabs a broom to sweep up too!

"I can show kindness
like Piper!"

Piper is very kind to baby Winston.

She watches as his kind
heart grows and grows.

She is happy helping out her little
brother. He is learning daily
from the kindness Piper shows.

Being kind can bring
happiness, not just to you.

Sharing kindness can help
others grow their hearts too!

Kindness changes the world,
and it helps those you know.

So show kindness like Piper,
wherever you go!

Show Kindness Like Piper:

1. Help mom with a chore.
2. Open the door for someone.
3. Give a compliment.
4. Help set the dinner table.
5. Bring flowers to your teacher.
6. Tell someone how much you love them.
7. Invite someone new to play on the playground.
8. Clean up your room without being asked.
9. Share with someone at school, a sibling or new friend.
10. Donate toys and books to a local place in need.

Complete this checklist and share it on social media. Tag us on Facebook and Instagram @piperfoxco or submit a picture by heading to piperfoxco.com.

PHOTO BY EMILY CHIDESTER

The Real Piper Fox

Piper is REAL! She is a three-year-old Shiba Inu who looks like a fox, which is why she is called Piper Fox! She has a younger Shiba Inu brother, Winston, and baby human brother, Beckett. Piper lives with her mom, dad, and two brothers in Charlotte, North Carolina. Her favorite things to do include chewing on toys, naps on the couch, and long walks with her mom and dad. Piper is known for her sweet personality and loving ways. She truly is the kindest pup!

Shop the Kindness Store
piperfoxco.com

Made in the USA
Monee, IL
05 November 2026

67985534R00021

Made in the USA
Monee, IL
05 November 2026

67985534R00021